BÚKOLLA

An Icelandic Fairy Tale
from the collected works
of Jón Árnason

Once upon a time, a man and a woman lived on a small farm. They had one son but held no great affection for him. They three were the only souls who dwelled there. The man and woman had but one creature, a single cow.

Her name was Búkolla.

One day, the cow bore a calf, and the woman kept vigil over her. But once the cow had borne and recovered from the delivery, the woman went back inside the cottage. She returned a short time later to call on the cow, but it had vanished. Both the man and woman commenced a search for her, delving far and wide, but in vain.

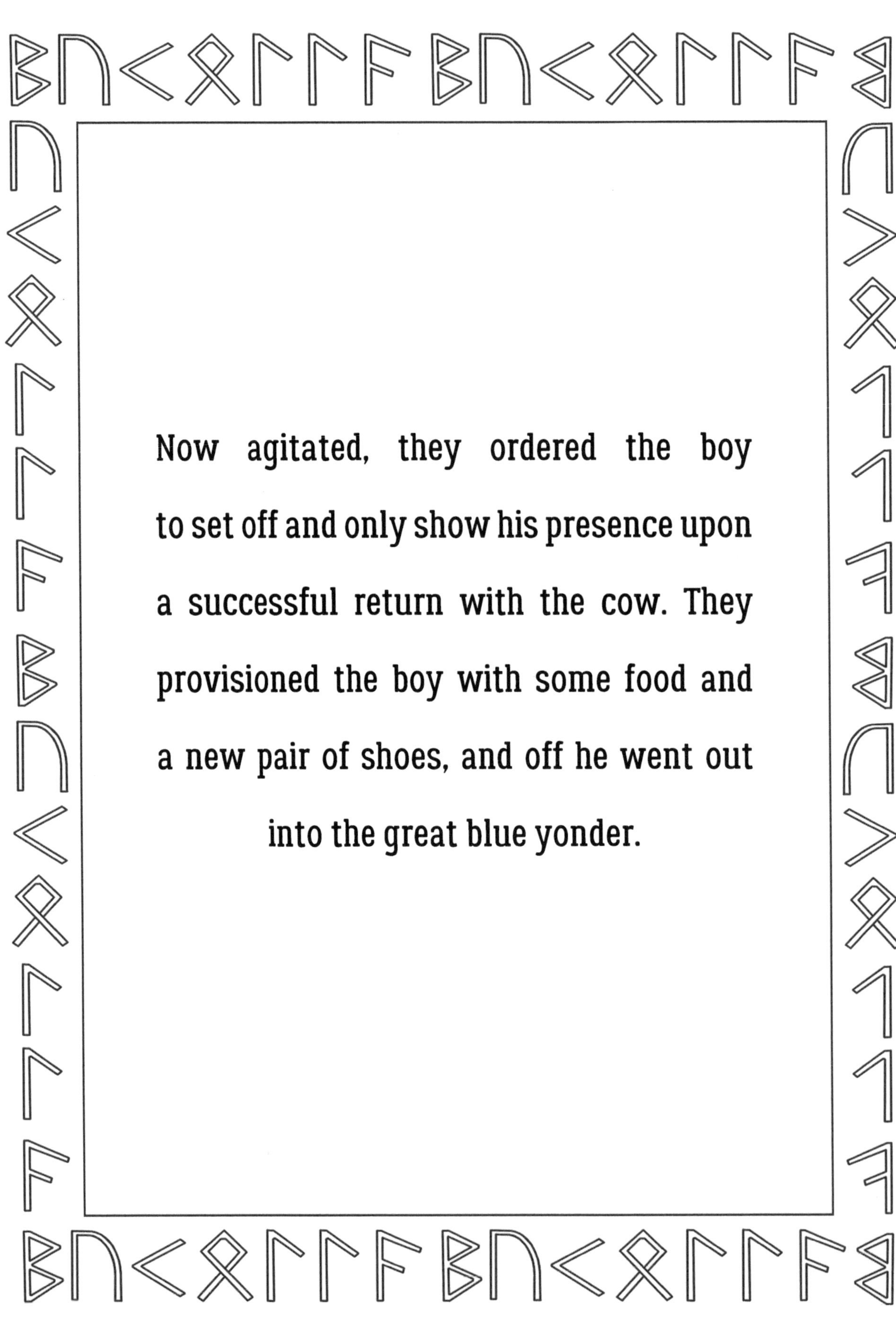

Now agitated, they ordered the boy to set off and only show his presence upon a successful return with the cow. They provisioned the boy with some food and a new pair of shoes, and off he went out into the great blue yonder.

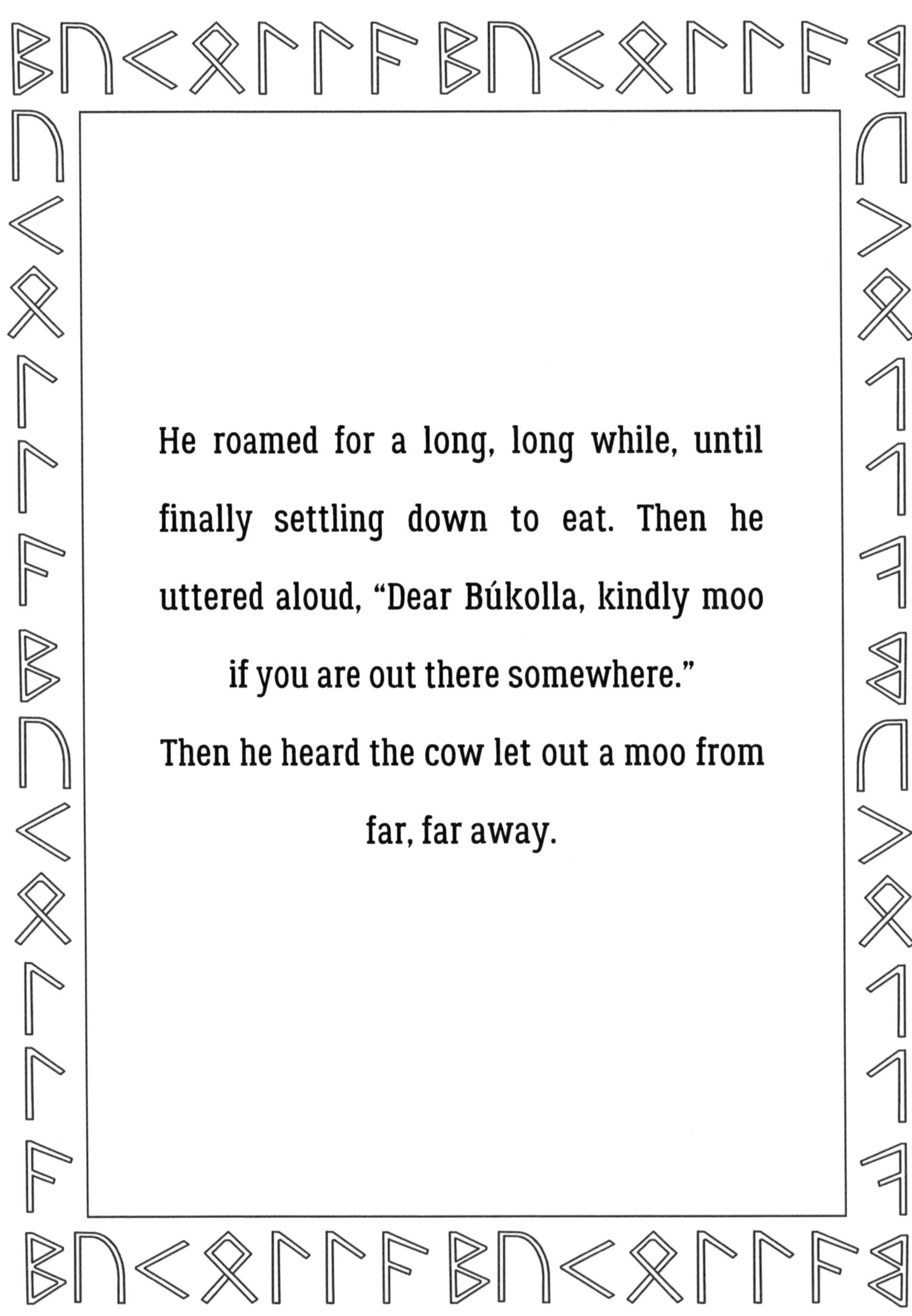

He roamed for a long, long while, until finally settling down to eat. Then he uttered aloud, “Dear Búkolla, kindly moo if you are out there somewhere.”

Then he heard the cow let out a moo from far, far away.

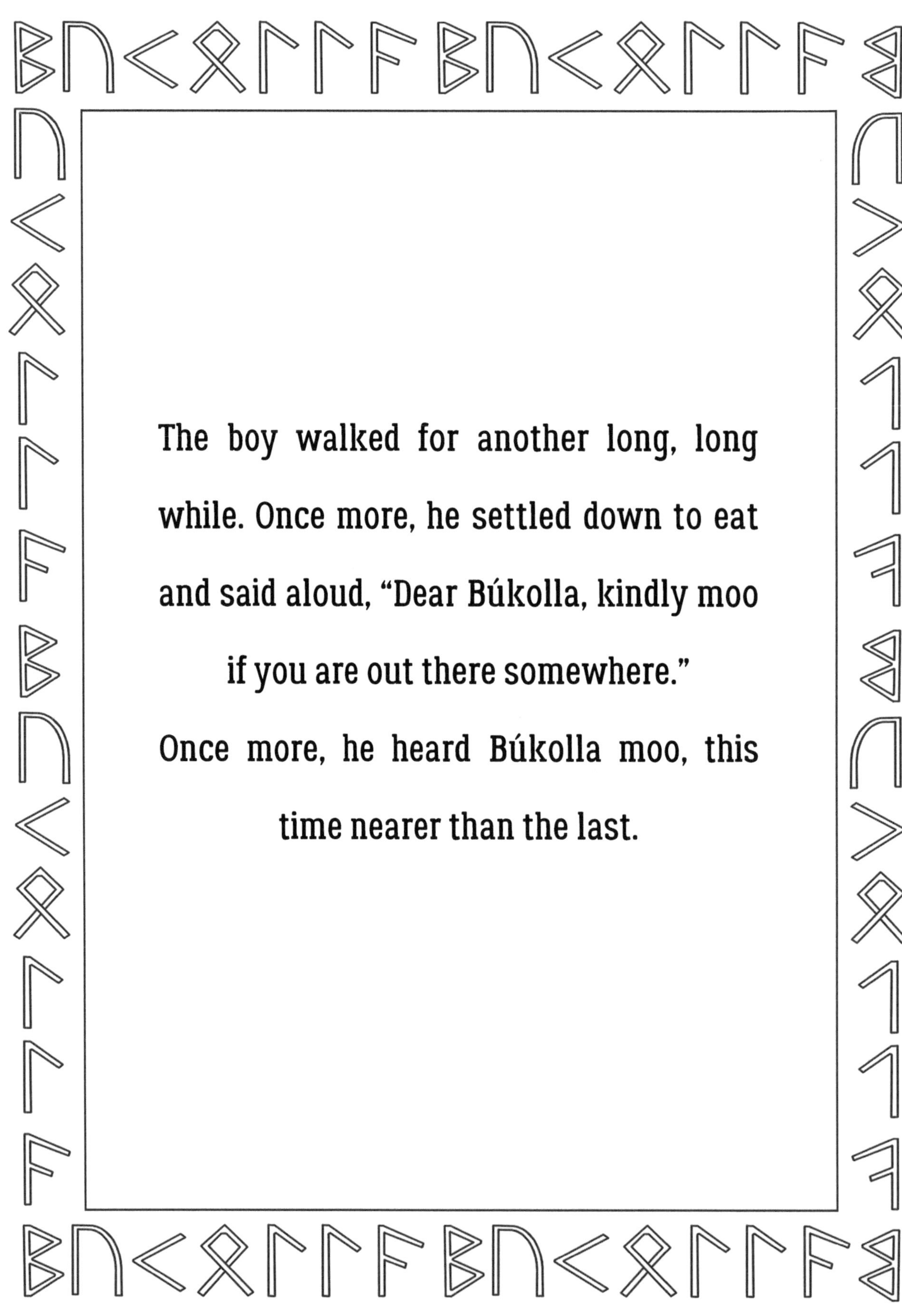

The boy walked for another long, long while. Once more, he settled down to eat and said aloud, “Dear Búkolla, kindly moo if you are out there somewhere.”

Once more, he heard Búkolla moo, this time nearer than the last.

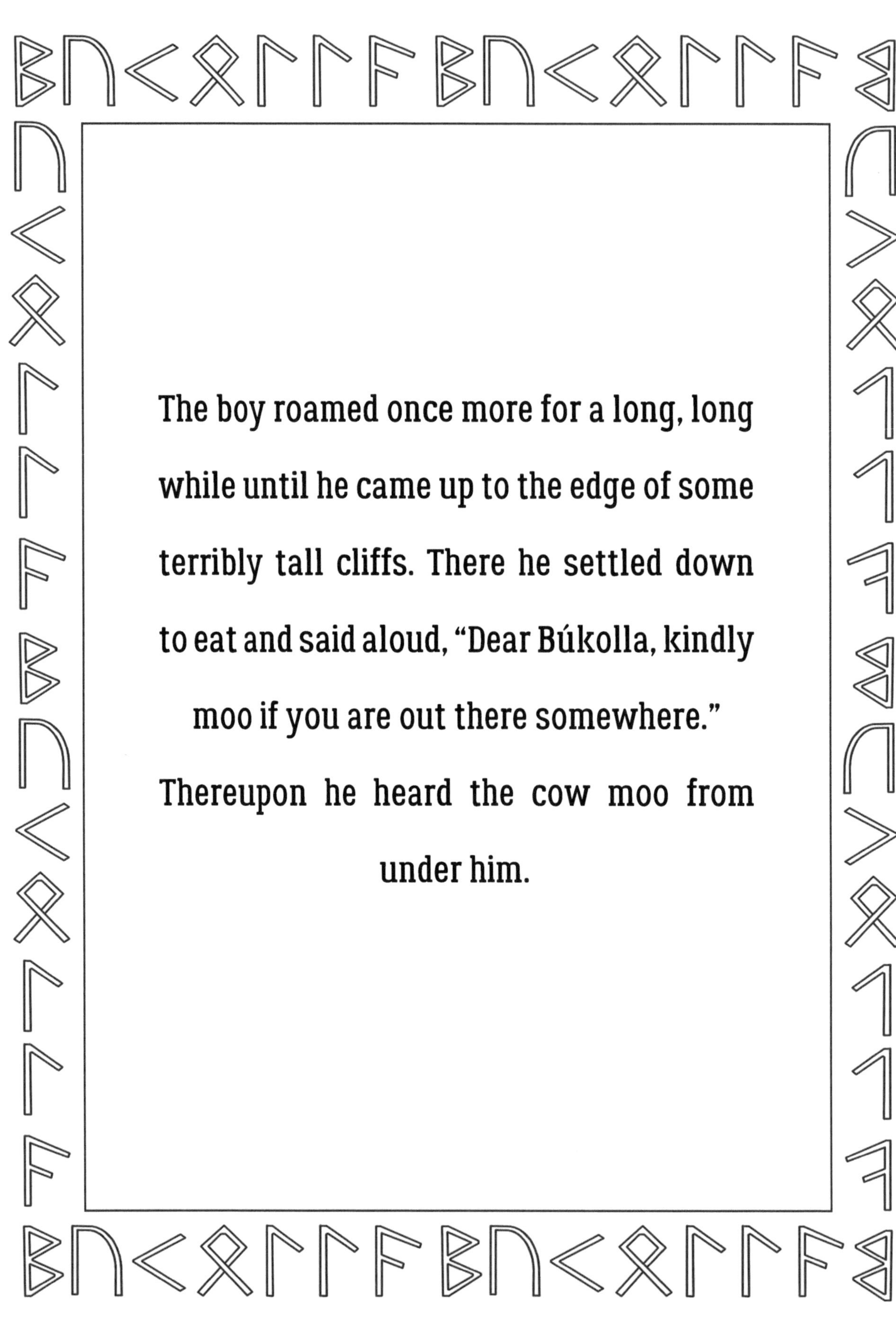

The boy roamed once more for a long, long while until he came up to the edge of some terribly tall cliffs. There he settled down to eat and said aloud, “Dear Búkolla, kindly moo if you are out there somewhere.” Thereupon he heard the cow moo from under him.

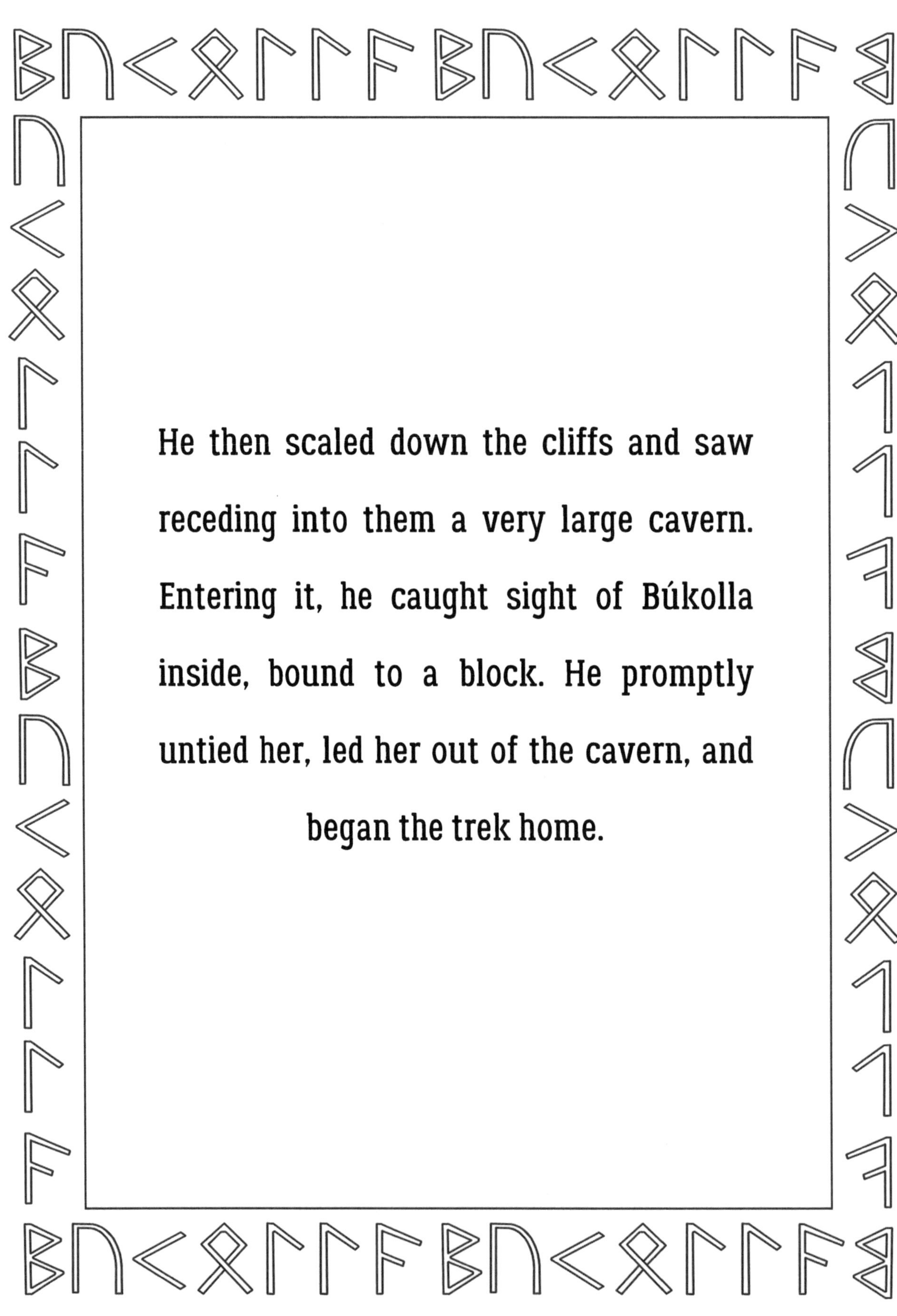

He then scaled down the cliffs and saw receding into them a very large cavern. Entering it, he caught sight of Búkolla inside, bound to a block. He promptly untied her, led her out of the cavern, and began the trek home.

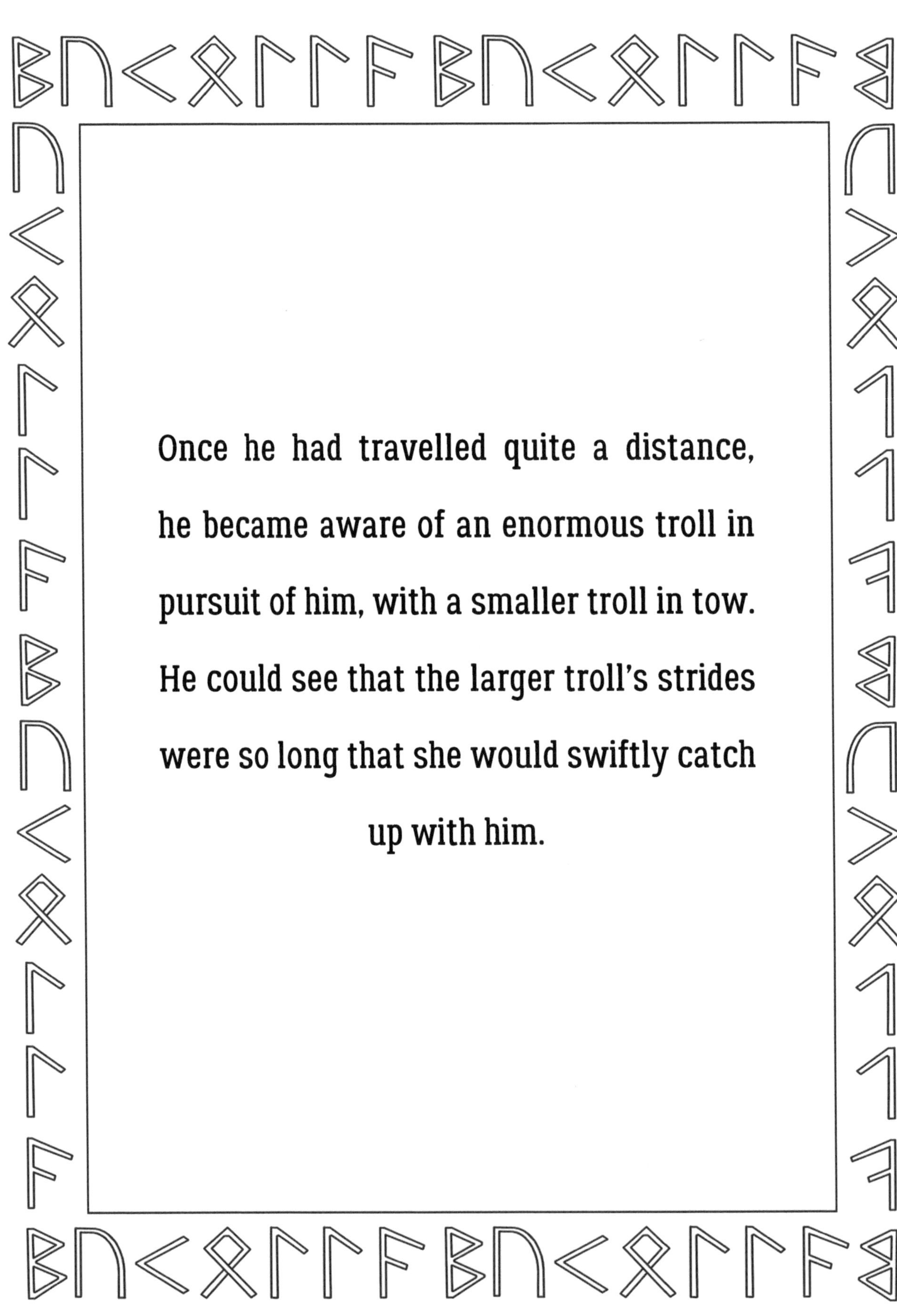

Once he had travelled quite a distance, he became aware of an enormous troll in pursuit of him, with a smaller troll in tow. He could see that the larger troll's strides were so long that she would swiftly catch up with him.

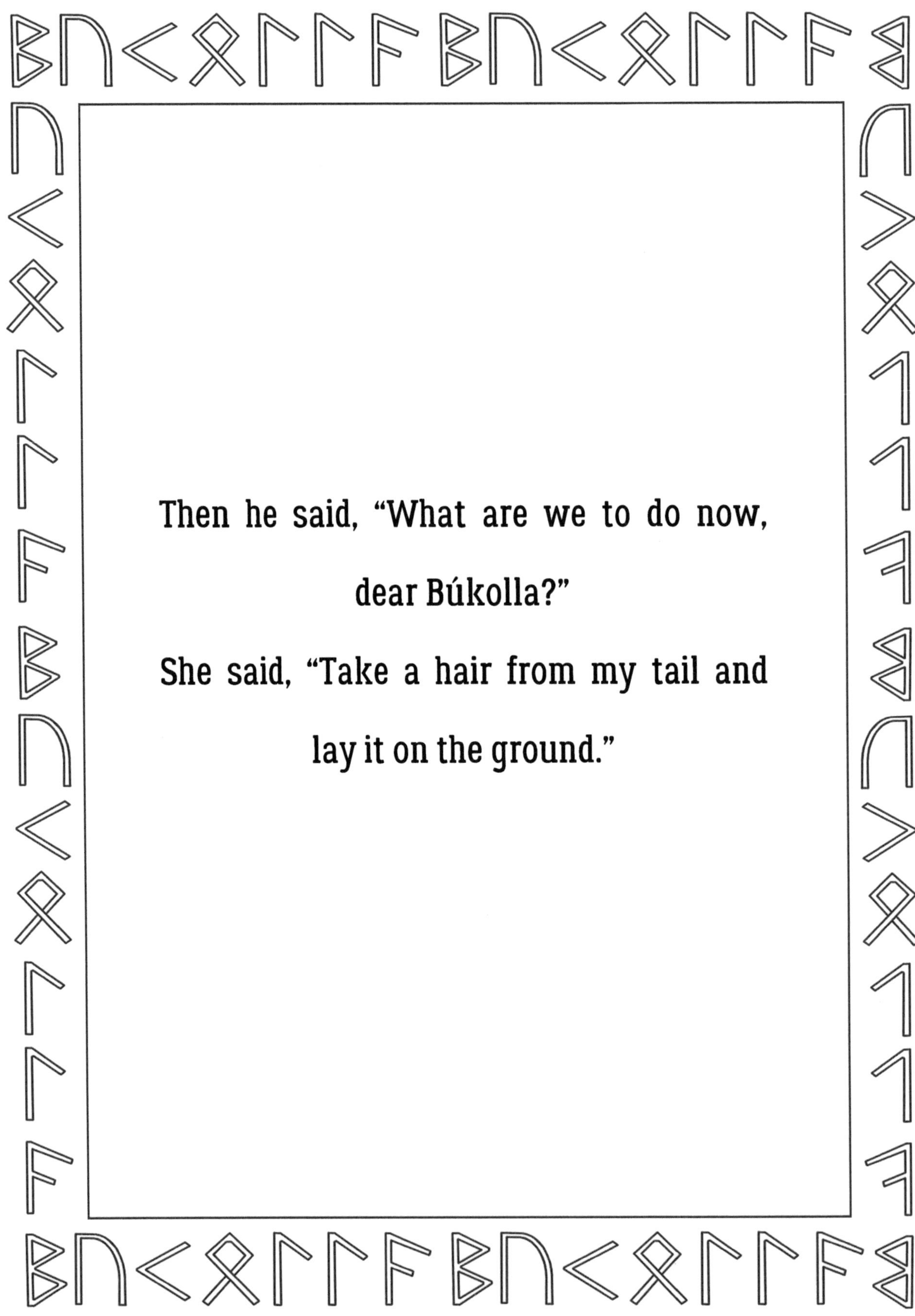

Then he said, “What are we to do now, dear Búkolla?”

She said, “Take a hair from my tail and lay it on the ground.”

This he did. Thereafter the cow spoke to the hair, “I do enspell and charm as well, for you to become a river so vast that only the soaring birds may cross you.”

That same moment did the hair turn into an enormous river.

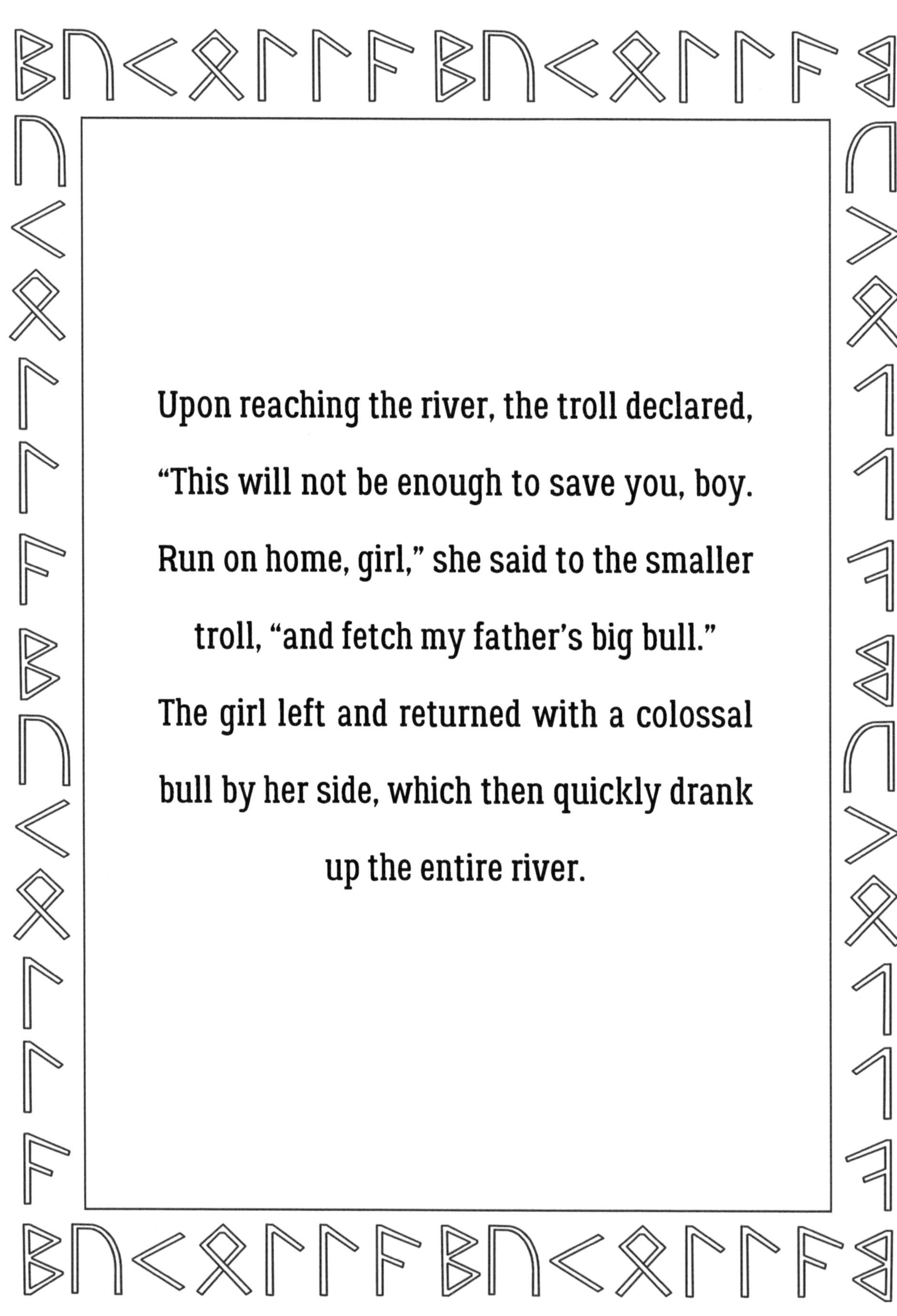

Upon reaching the river, the troll declared, “This will not be enough to save you, boy. Run on home, girl,” she said to the smaller troll, “and fetch my father’s big bull.” The girl left and returned with a colossal bull by her side, which then quickly drank up the entire river.

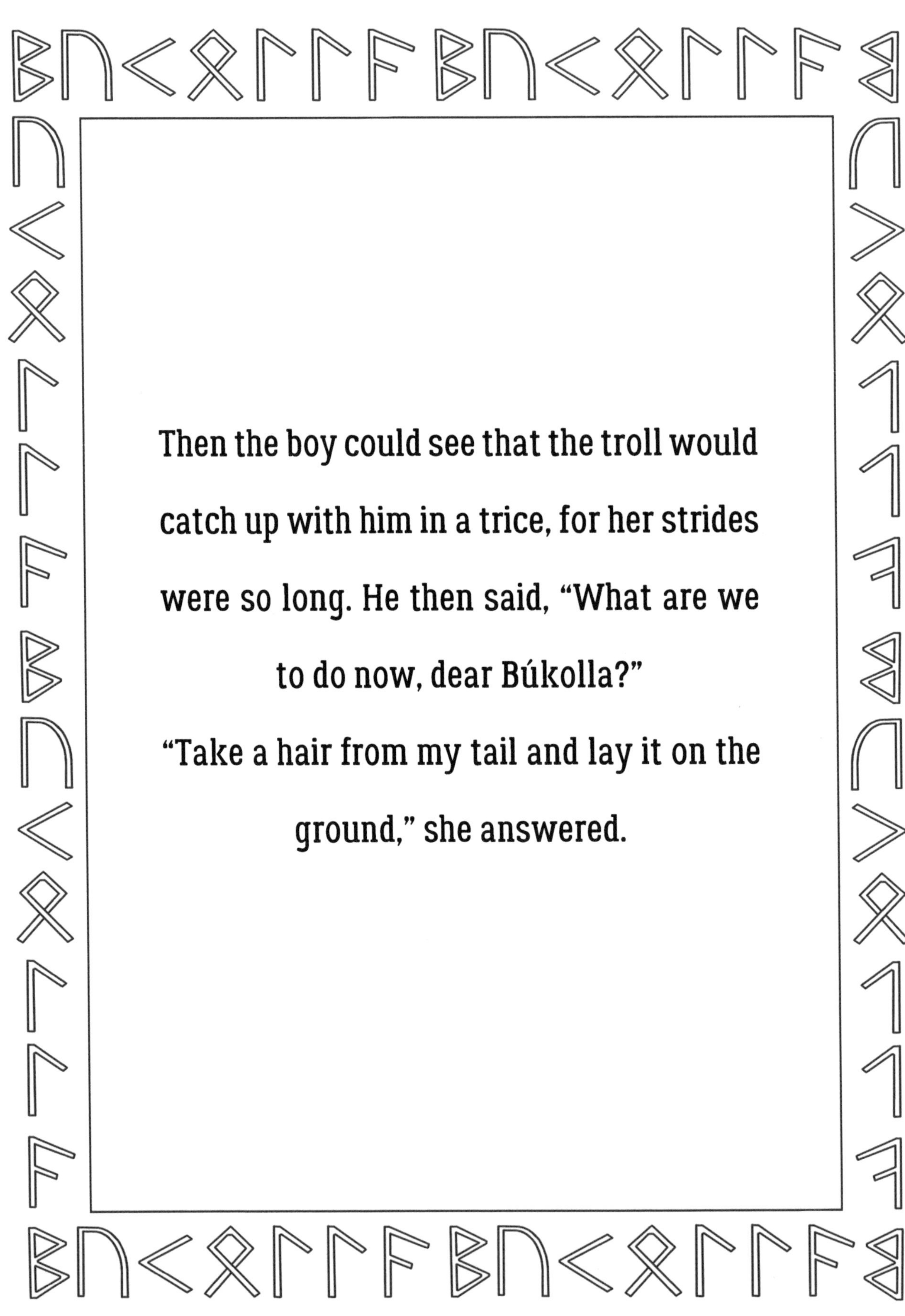

Then the boy could see that the troll would catch up with him in a trice, for her strides were so long. He then said, “What are we to do now, dear Búkolla?”

“Take a hair from my tail and lay it on the ground,” she answered.

This he did. Thereafter Búkolla spoke to the hair, “I do enspell and charm as well, that you be made a flame so tall that only the soaring birds may rise above you.” And right away did the hair come to be a blazing inferno.

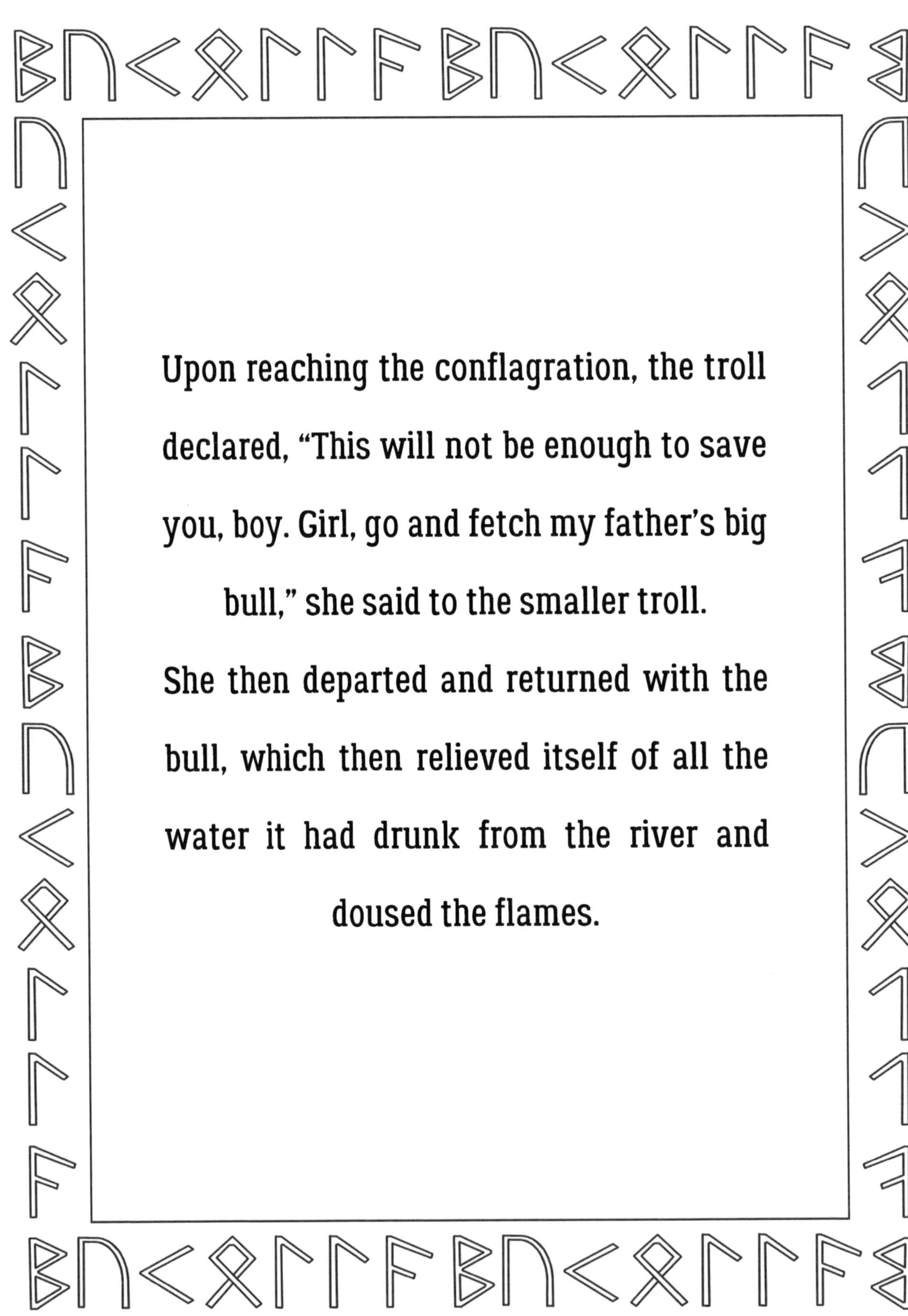

Upon reaching the conflagration, the troll declared, “This will not be enough to save you, boy. Girl, go and fetch my father’s big bull,” she said to the smaller troll.

She then departed and returned with the bull, which then relieved itself of all the water it had drunk from the river and doused the flames.

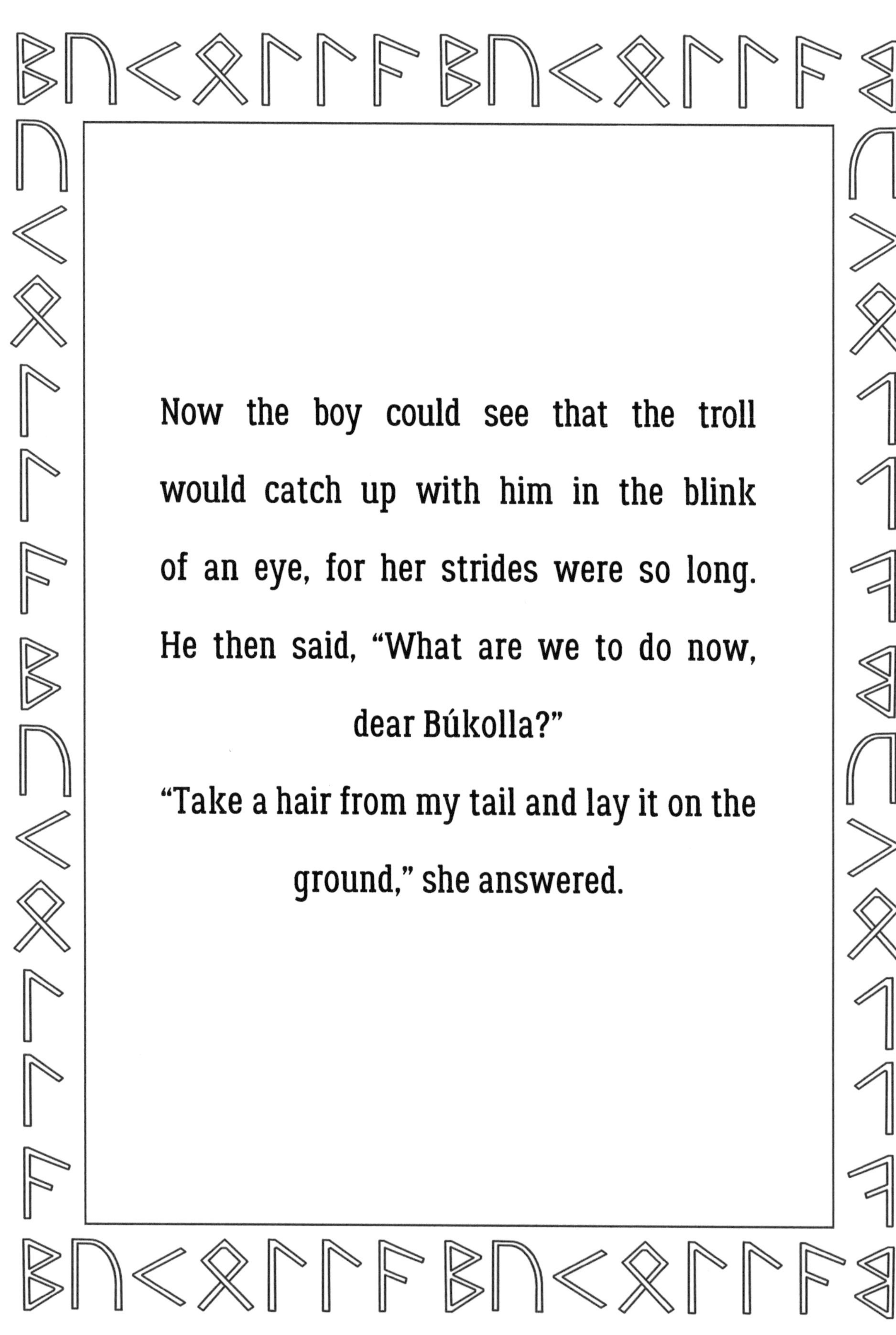

Now the boy could see that the troll would catch up with him in the blink of an eye, for her strides were so long. He then said, “What are we to do now, dear Búkolla?”

“Take a hair from my tail and lay it on the ground,” she answered.

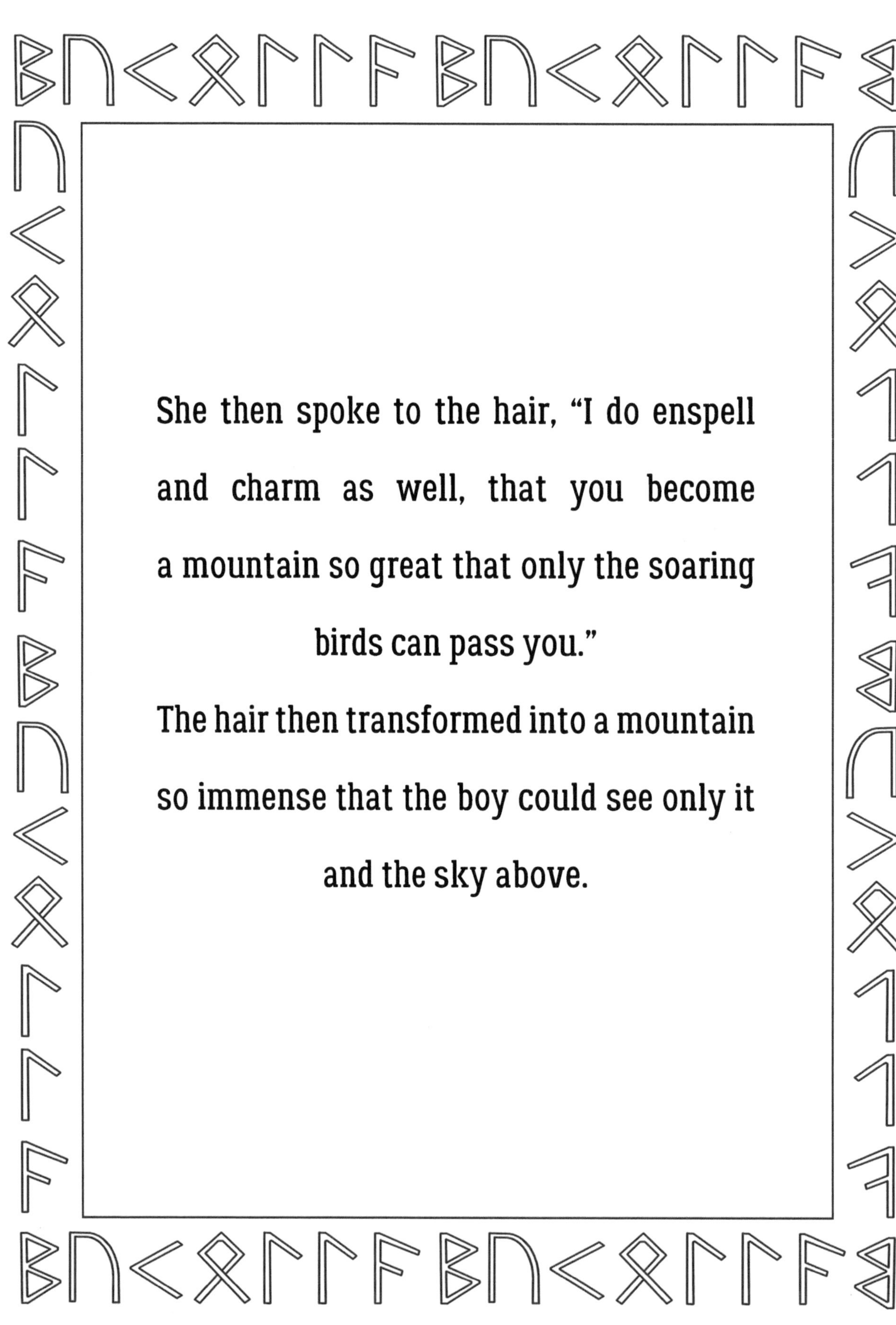

She then spoke to the hair, "I do enspell and charm as well, that you become a mountain so great that only the soaring birds can pass you."

The hair then transformed into a mountain so immense that the boy could see only it and the sky above.

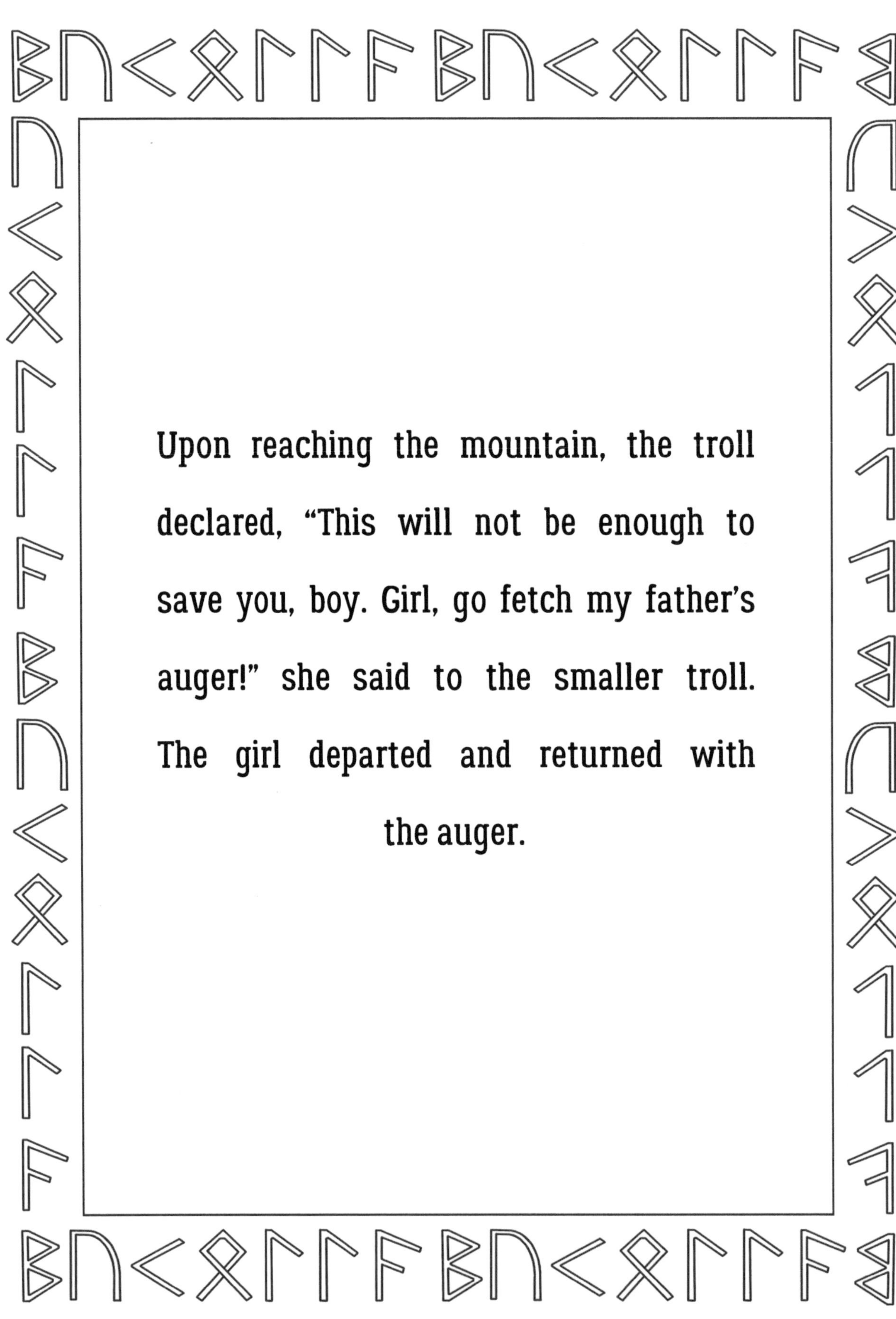

Upon reaching the mountain, the troll declared, “This will not be enough to save you, boy. Girl, go fetch my father’s auger!” she said to the smaller troll. The girl departed and returned with the auger.

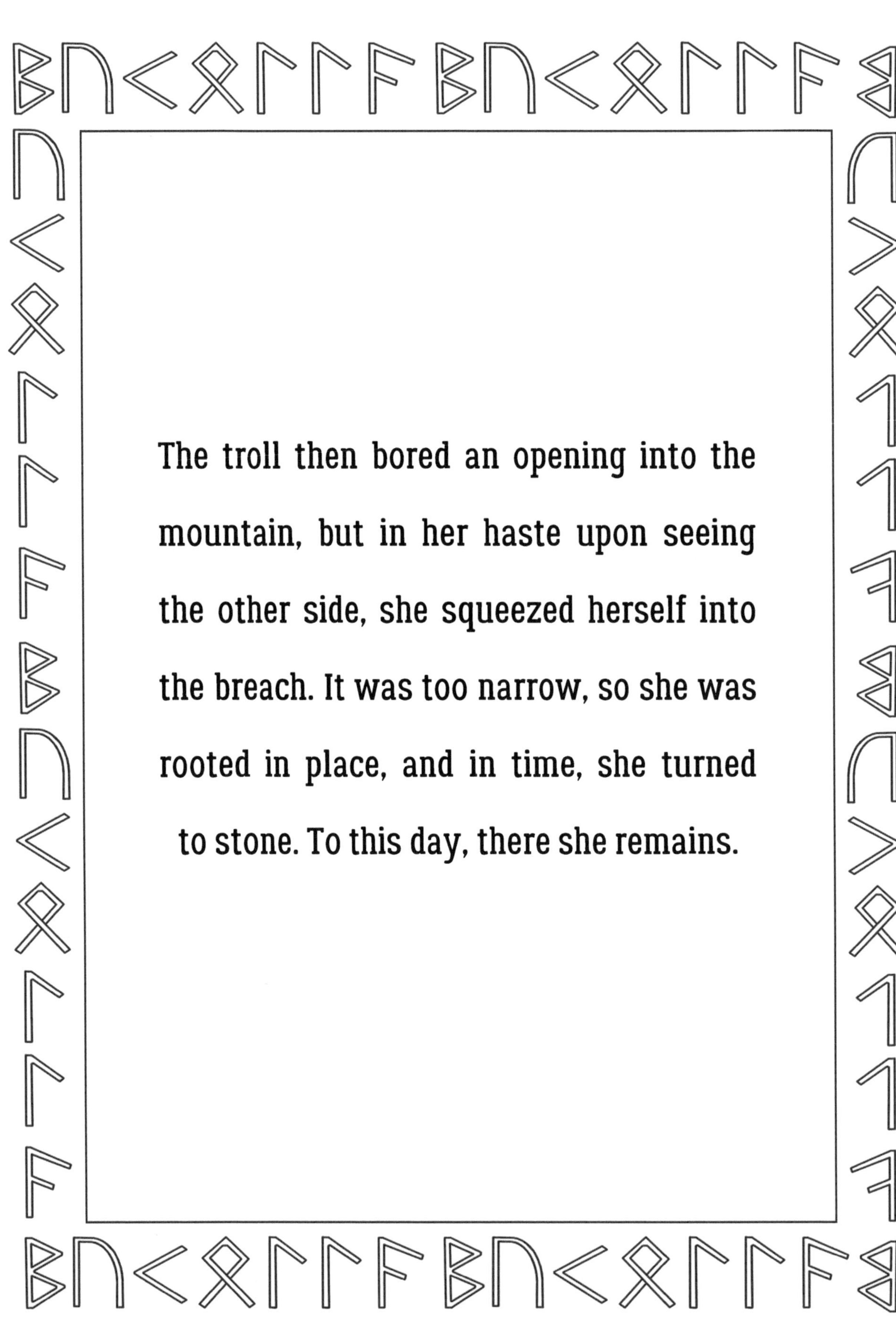

The troll then bored an opening into the mountain, but in her haste upon seeing the other side, she squeezed herself into the breach. It was too narrow, so she was rooted in place, and in time, she turned to stone. To this day, there she remains.

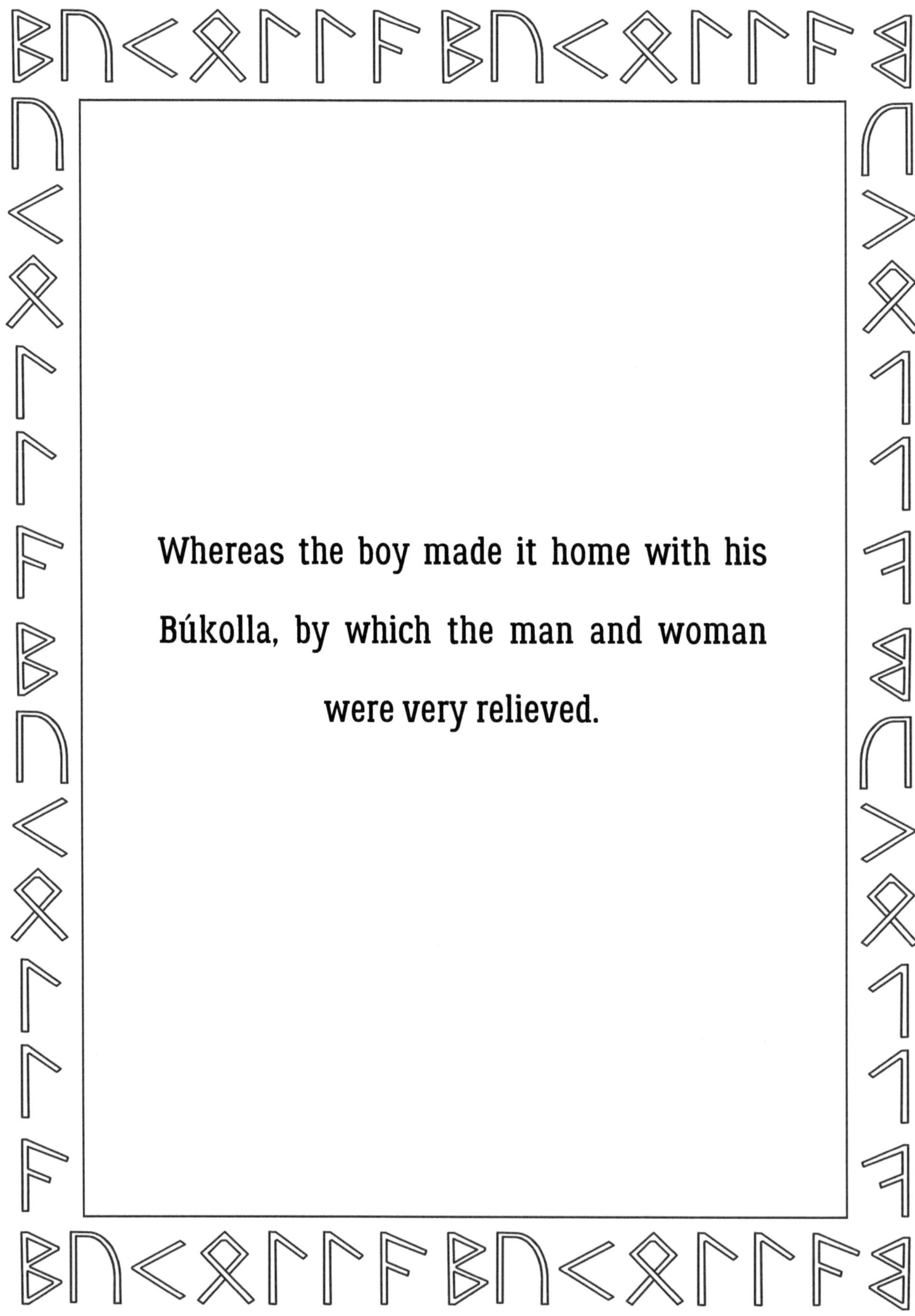

Whereas the boy made it home with his Búkolla, by which the man and woman were very relieved.

Búkolla

An Icelandic Adventure from the collected works of Jón Árnason

English translation: © Dmitri Antonov

Layout: Elena Strelnikova

Printing: Amazon

ISBN: 978-9935-9449-4-8

Antonov Publishing 2021

www.battlingauthor.com

www.ingramcontent.com/pod-product-compliance
Ingram Content Group UK Ltd.
Pitfield, Milton Keynes, MK11 3LW, UK
UKHW061029310726
14090UKWH00027B/366

* 9 7 8 9 9 3 5 9 4 4 9 4 8 *